mapping
AUSTRALIA

Gareth Stevens
Publishing

By Janey Levy

Please visit our website, www.garethstevens.com. For a free color catalog of all our high-quality books, call toll free 1-800-542-2595 or fax 1-877-542-2596.

Library of Congress Cataloging-in-Publication Data

Levy, Janey.
 Mapping Australia / Janey Levy.
    pages cm. — (Mapping the world)
 Includes index.
 ISBN 978-1-4339-9105-9 (pbk.)
 ISBN 978-1-4339-9106-6 (6-pack)
 ISBN 978-1-4339-9104-2 (library binding)
 1. Maps—Australia—Juvenile literature. 2. Cartography—Australia—Juvenile literature. 3. Australia—Description and travel—Juvenile literature. I. Title.
 GA1681.L48 2014
 919.4—dc23

                                        2012049129

First Edition

Published in 2014 by
Gareth Stevens Publishing
111 East 14th Street, Suite 349
New York, NY 10003

Designer: Katelyn E. Reynolds
Editor: Kristen Rajczak

Photo credits: Cover, p. 1 (photo) kwest/Shutterstock.com; cover, p. 1 (map) Uwe Dedering/Wikipedia.com; cover, pp. 1–24 (banner) kanate/Shutterstock.com; cover, pp. 1–24 (series elements and cork background) iStockphoto/Thinkstock.com; p. 5 The World Factbook/CIA; p. 7 (inset) robert paul van beets/Shutterstock.com; p. 7 (main) Hans Braxmeier/Wikipedia.com; p. 9 (inset) deb22/Shutterstock.com; p. 9 (main) ESA; p. 11 (inset) Paul Chesley/Stone/Getty Images; pp. 11 (main), 15 (main) SonNy cZ/Wikipedia.com; p. 13 (inset) Lonely Planet Images/Getty Images; p. 13 (main) John Foxx/Stockbyte/Thinkstock.com; p. 15 (inset) Ted Aljibe/AFP/Getty Images; pp. 17, 19 (inset right) iStockphoto/Thinkstock.com; p. 19 (inset left) Hemera/Thinkstock.com; p. 19 (main) Commonwealth of Australia 2013 on behalf of ICSM; p. 21 dalmingo/Shutterstock.com.

Printed in the United States of America

CPSIA compliance information: Batch #CS13GS: For further information contact Gareth Stevens, New York, New York at 1-800-542-2595.

CONTENTS

DEC 3 1 2013

Words in the glossary appear in **bold** type the first time they are used in the text.

THE ISLAND CONTINENT

When you think of Australia, do you picture kangaroos and koalas? Australia's unusual animals make it special. But it's special for other reasons, too. It's called the island **continent** because it's both a small continent and a large island. It's the flattest and second-driest continent, and the only continent that's also a country!

Australia lies between the Pacific and the Indian Oceans in the Southern **Hemisphere**. The capital is Canberra. Australia's sunshine, unusual animals, and special land features draw millions of visitors every year.

Where in the World?

Australia is sometimes called the Land Down Under because the entire country lies south of the **equator**.

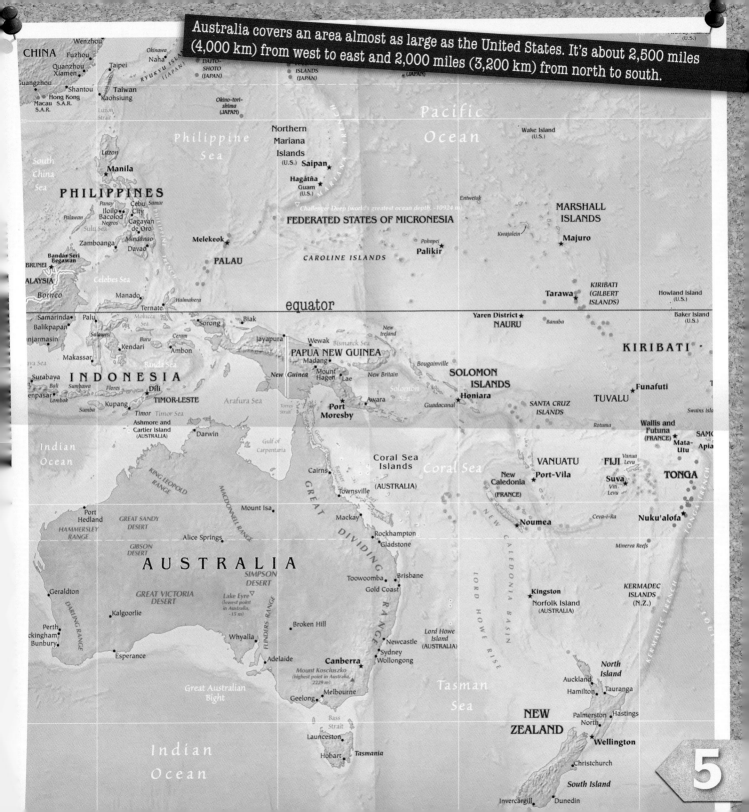

Australia covers an area almost as large as the United States. It's about 2,500 miles (4,000 km) from west to east and 2,000 miles (3,200 km) from north to south.

CHINA
Wenzhou
Fuzhou
Quanzhou
Xiamen
Guangzhou
Shantou
Hong Kong
Macau S.A.R.
S.A.R.
Taipei
Okinawa
Naha
RYUKYU ISLANDS (JAPAN)
Taiwan
Kaohsiung
Okino-tori-shima (JAPAN)
DAITO-SHOTO (JAPAN)
ISLANDS (JAPAN)
(JAPAN)

Pacific
Ocean

Wake Island (U.S.)

Luzon

Manila

South China Sea

Philippine Sea

Northern
Mariana
Islands
(U.S.) **Saipan**
Hagåtña
Guam
(U.S.)

MARSHALL
ISLANDS

Entwetak

PHILIPPINES
Panay
Iloilo Cebu Samar
Bacolod City
Negros Cagayan
de Oro

Challenger Deep (world's greatest ocean depth, -10924 m)

Kwajalein

Majuro

Zamboanga
Mindanao
Davao
Melekeok
FEDERATED STATES OF MICRONESIA
Palikir
Pohnpei

Sulu Sea
Palawan

BRUNEI
Bandar Seri
Begawan
PALAU
CAROLINE ISLANDS

KIRIBATI (GILBERT ISLANDS)
Howland Island (U.S.)

ALAYSIA
Celebes Sea
Manado
Halmahera
Ternate
Tarawa

Borneo
Samarinda
Balikpapan
njarmasin
Palu
Molucca Sea
Sulawesi
Buru
Ceram
Sorong
Biak
equator
Yaren District ★
NAURU
Banaba
Baker Island (U.S.)

Makassar
Kendari
Ambon
Jayapura
Wewak
New
Ireland
KIRIBATI

Java Sea
Surabaya
Bali
Sumbawa
Flores
Dili
PAPUA NEW GUINEA
Madang
Bismarck Sea
Bougainville
SOLOMON
ISLANDS
Funafuti

enpasar
Lombok
Kupang
TIMOR-LESTE
Timor
Timor Sea
New Guinea
Mount
Hagen
Lae
New Britain
Awara
Solomon Sea
Honiara
Guadacanal
SANTA CRUZ
ISLANDS
TUVALU

INDONESIA
Samba
Torres
Strait
Port Moresby
Rotuma
Wallis and Futuna (FRANCE)
SAMO
Mata-Utu
Apia

Arafura Sea
Ashmore and
Cartier Island
(AUSTRALIA)
Darwin

Indian Ocean

Gulf of Carpentaria

Coral Sea
Islands

VANUATU
Port-Vila
Vanua
Levu
FIJI
Viti
Levu

TONGA

Cairns

Suva

Coral Sea

New
Caledonia
(FRANCE)

KING LEOPOLD
RANGE

MACDONNELL RANGE

Townsville

(AUSTRALIA)

Ceva-i-Ra

Nuku'alofa

Port
Hedland
HAMMERSLEY
RANGE
GREAT SANDY
DESERT
Mount Isa
Mackay
Noumea

GREAT
DIVIDING

Minerva Reefs

Geraldton
GIBSON
DESERT
Alice Springs
Rockhampton
Gladstone

KERMADEC
ISLANDS
(N.Z.)

AUSTRALIA
SIMPSON
DESERT
RANGE

Kalgoorlie
GREAT VICTORIA
DESERT
Lake Eyre ▽
(lowest point
in Australia,
-15 m)
Toowoomba
Brisbane
Gold Coast

Kingston
Norfolk Island
(AUSTRALIA)

Perth
ckingham
Bunbury
DARLING RANGE
Broken Hill
FLINDERS RANGE
Newcastle
Lord Howe
Island
(AUSTRALIA)

Esperance
Whyalla
Adelaide
Mount Kosciuszko
(highest point in Australia,
2229 m)
Canberra
Sydney
Wollongong

*Great Australian
Bight*
Geelong
Melbourne

*Tasman
Sea*

North
Island
Auckland
Tauranga
Hamilton

Bass
Strait
Launceston
**NEW
ZEALAND**
Palmerston
North
Hastings

*Indian
Ocean*
Hobart
Tasmania
Wellington

Christchurch

South Island

Invercargill
Dunedin

HIGHLANDS AND LOWLANDS

If you travel across Australia from east to west, you pass through the country's three main regions, or areas. The eastern highlands have hills, mountains, **plateaus**, and lots of people. The region also receives lots of rain.

The central lowlands are flat and dry. Rivers appear after heavy rains, but it doesn't rain often. There are no large cities here.

The western plateau covers two-thirds of Australia. Deserts fill much of the region. Two large cities are located along the coast.

Where in the World?

The area called the Outback covers much of the central lowlands and western plateau. It's hot, dry, and has few people.

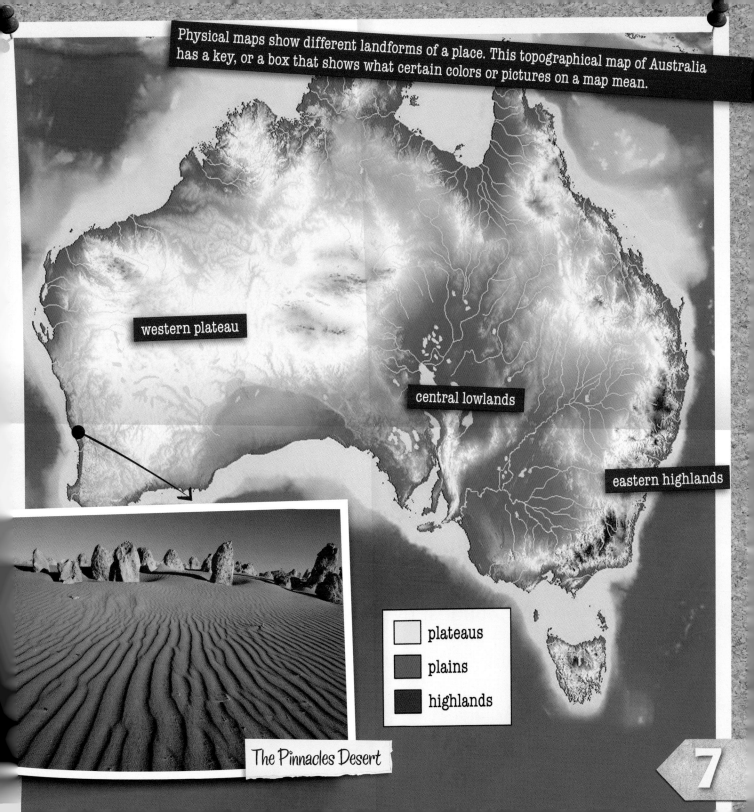

Physical maps show different landforms of a place. This topographical map of Australia has a key, or a box that shows what certain colors or pictures on a map mean.

western plateau

central lowlands

eastern highlands

plateaus
plains
highlands

The Pinnacles Desert

7

MOUNTAINS, DESERTS, ROCKS, AND RIVERS

Among Australia's many special land features are the Australian Alps in the eastern highlands. The continent's highest mountain, Mount Kosciuszko (kah-see-UHS-koh), is found here. It rises 7,310 feet (2,228 m).

Deserts fill Australia's famous Outback. Huge rocks rise above them in places. Uluru, the most famous, is **sacred** for Australia's **Aborigines** (aa-buh-RIH-juh-neez).

Many rivers are dry for part of the year. The longest river that always has water is the Murray River. From the Alps, it flows west for about 1,550 miles (2,500 km).

Where in the World?

Winds blow the desert sands and create giant **dunes**. Some dunes are more than 200 miles (320 km) long!

8

One of Australia's most famous features isn't on land—it's under the ocean. Stretching about 1,400 miles (2,300 km) along the northeastern coast is the world's largest **coral reef**—the Great Barrier Reef.

Great Barrier Reef

Great Barrier Reef

9

AUSTRALIA'S PEOPLE

Like the United States, Australia is a melting pot, with a population made up of people from many places. Australia's native people are called Aborigines. They first came to Australia more than 50,000 years ago! European settlers began to arrive in 1788. Recently, many settlers have come from Asia.

More than three-fourths of Australia's people live in the crowded southeastern part of the country. Most of the rest live along the northeastern and southwestern coasts. Few people try to live in the hot, dry Outback.

Where in the World?

Less than one-fifth of the people in Australia are 14 years old or younger. More than two-thirds are between 15 and 64 years old.

Aboriginal men

Australia's Population Density
(km sq)

- 0–1
- 1–10
- 10–100
- 100–1000
- 1000–10000

CITY SOCIETY

Do you prefer city life or country life? Most Australians prefer city life. Of the country's almost 22 million people, about 9 out of every 10 live in cities or towns.

The continent's biggest cities, Sydney and Melbourne, are on the southeastern coast. About 4 million people live in Sydney, and about 3.5 million live in Melbourne. Perth, the largest city on the west coast, has about 1.5 million people. Canberra, the nation's capital, has only about 330,000.

Where in the World?

Most Australians live within about 31 miles (50 km) of the coast. All the largest cities are on the coast.

Crows Nest
To Ku-Ring-Gai-Chase National Park
reenwich
North Sydney
Waverton
Mosman
Neutral Bay
Cremorne
0 — 2 km
0 — 1 mile
Sydney Harbour National Park
Watsons Bay
McMahons Point
Nielsen Park
Goat Island
Shark Island
Vaucluse
grove
The Rocks
Sydney Opera House
Sydney Harbour
Darling Harbour
Circular Quay
Botanic Gardens
Clarke Island
int Piper
main
Macquarie St
Art Gallery of NSW
The Domain
Dover Heights
Pyrmont
Rose Bay
Glebe
Darling Harbour
Hyde Park
Kings Cross
Darling Point
North Bondi
Darlinghurst
Bellevue Hill
Haymarket
Paddington
Woollahra
Chippendale
Surry Hills
Sydney Football Stadium
Sydney Cricket Ground
Bondi
Bondi Beach
To Royal National Park

13

RICHES FROM THE LAND

Australia is rich in **natural resources**. About half the land is farmland. However, most of it is dry land where sheep and cattle feed on grass and bushes. Only about one-tenth of the farmland is used to grow crops.

Eucalyptus trees fill the forests of the eastern highlands. Their hard wood is used to make paper and furniture.

The land holds valued **minerals**, too. Australia is one of the world's top gold producers. Silver, copper, and tin are also found there.

Where in the World?

Australia has lots of underground water. But most of it is too salty for people to drink or use to water crops.

Natural resource maps can show where certain crops are grown as well as the location of minerals. Use this map to find where gold is often found in Australia.

Australian gold nugget

Northern Territory

Queensland

Western Australia

South Australia

New South Wales

Victoria

Australia's Major Gold Producing Regions

Tasmania

KANGAROOS, KOALAS, AND MORE

Australia is especially famous for its unusual animals. Perhaps the best known are kangaroos and koalas, which are both marsupials. But did you know Australia has many other marsupials? About 150 kinds live there! They include wallabies, which are small kangaroos, and wombats, which live in holes in the ground.

About 700 kinds of birds live in Australia, including the only black swans in the world. The emu and the cassowary are so large they can't fly, just like the ostrich.

Where in the World?

Australia has about 140 kinds of snakes, most of which are poisonous. The taipan and the tiger snake are two of the deadliest snakes in the world!

These koalas are marsupials, a kind of **mammal** that has a pouch in which to carry its babies.

17

WATTLES AND EUCALYPTS

What are wattles? Well, that's the name Australians use for acacias (uh-KAY-shuhz), one of the continent's main kinds of plants. These plants bear seeds in pods and often have colorful flowers. About 700 kinds grow across Australia! They're tall trees in wet areas and shorter **shrubs** in dry areas.

"Eucalypts" is the name Australians uses for eucalyptuses, the most common type of plant in the country. Their narrow, leathery leaves have scented oil. Like acacias, they can be tall trees or short shrubs.

Where in the World?

Saltbushes grow in dry parts of the country where livestock are raised. Their salty leaves are excellent food for cattle.

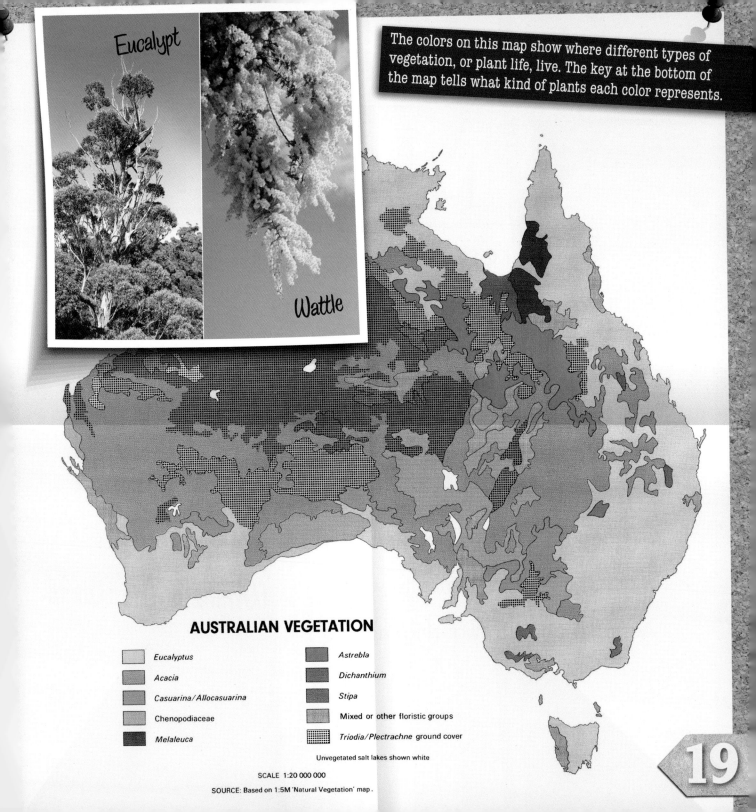

Eucalypt

Wattle

The colors on this map show where different types of vegetation, or plant life, live. The key at the bottom of the map tells what kind of plants each color represents.

AUSTRALIAN VEGETATION

Eucalyptus

Acacia

Casuarina/Allocasuarina

Chenopodiaceae

Melaleuca

Astrebla

Dichanthium

Stipa

Mixed or other floristic groups

Triodia/Plectrachne ground cover

Unvegetated salt lakes shown white

SCALE 1:20 000 000

SOURCE: Based on 1:5M 'Natural Vegetation' map.

19

"WALTZING MATILDA"

"Waltzing Matilda" is Australia's most famous song. But it doesn't mean what you might think.

A "matilda" is a blanket roll, and "to waltz matilda" means "to tramp the roads," or to travel around the country. It's a fitting song for a land whose people love outdoor living and whose special features offer a sense of wonder and invite people to explore. Maybe one day you'll have a chance to visit Australia and go "waltzing matilda"!

Where in the World?

Would you visit the Australian wilderness? "Walkabout" tours are based on the Aborigine tradition of a person's journey to learn more about the land around them.

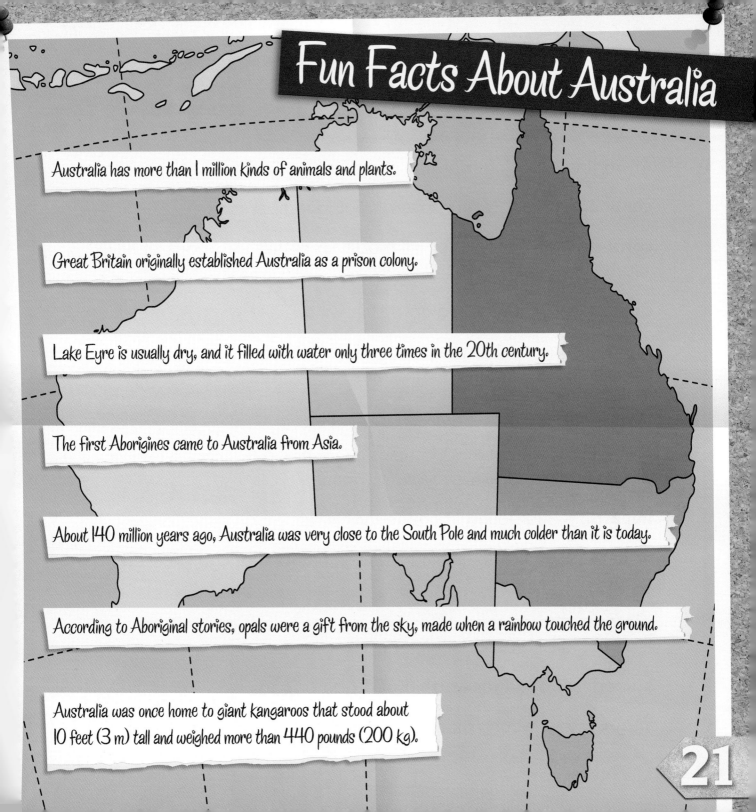

Fun Facts About Australia

Australia has more than 1 million kinds of animals and plants.

Great Britain originally established Australia as a prison colony.

Lake Eyre is usually dry, and it filled with water only three times in the 20th century.

The first Aborigines came to Australia from Asia.

About 140 million years ago, Australia was very close to the South Pole and much colder than it is today.

According to Aboriginal stories, opals were a gift from the sky, made when a rainbow touched the ground.

Australia was once home to giant kangaroos that stood about 10 feet (3 m) tall and weighed more than 440 pounds (200 kg).

GLOSSARY

Aborigine: a member of any of the original peoples of Australia

continent: one of Earth's seven great landmasses

coral reef: an underwater hill made up of the hard parts of tiny sea animals

dune: a hill of sand piled up by the wind

equator: an imaginary line around Earth that is the same distance from the North and the South Poles

hemisphere: one half of Earth

mammal: a warm-blooded animal that has a backbone and hair, breathes air, and feeds milk to its young

mineral: matter found in nature that is not living

natural resource: something found in nature that can be used by people

plateau: a large area of land that is flat on top and much higher than the land around it

sacred: set apart for worship of a god or gods

shrub: a low, woody plant

FOR MORE INFORMATION

Books

Bagley, Katie. *Australia*. Mankato, MN: Bridgestone Books, 2003.

Colson, Mary. *Australia*. Chicago, IL: Heinemann Library, 2012.

Kalman, Bobbie. *Spotlight on Australia*. New York, NY: Crabtree Publishing, 2008.

Websites

Australia
kids.nationalgeographic.com/kids/places/find/australia/
Read facts about Australia and see photos, videos, and more.

Fun Facts About Australia
www.2020site.org/fun-facts/Fun-Facts-About-Australia.html
Learn about Australia's language and climate, and discover a collection of fun facts about the country.

23

INDEX